STEP-BY-STEP
EXPERIMENTS WITH
SIMPLE MACHINES

By Gina Hagler

Illustrated by Bob Ostrom

The Child's World

Published by The Child's World®
1980 Lookout Drive • Mankato, MN 56003-1705
800-599-READ • www.childsworld.com

ACKNOWLEDGMENTS
The Child's World®: Mary Berendes, Publishing Director
The Design Lab: Design and production
Red Line Editorial: Editorial direction
Consultant: Dr. Peter Barnes, Assistant Scientist, Astronomy Dept.,
   University of Florida

ISBN 9781609735869
LCCN 2011940147

PHOTO CREDITS
Sylvie Bouchard/Dreamstime, cover; Pilar Echeverria/Dreamstime, cover,
back cover; Sergey Jarochkin/Shutterstock Images, 1, 8; James Steidl/
Shutterstock Images, 4; Tomo Jesenicnik/Dreamstime, 11; Sergei Chu-
makov/Shutterstock Images, 12; John Photon/Shutterstock Images, 17;
Shutterstock Images, 18; Paul Topp/Dreamstime, 23; Sergey Lavrentev/
Shutterstock Images, 24; Mike Weidman/Dreamstime, 28

Design elements: Pilar Echeverria/Dreamstime, Robisklp/Dreamstime,
Sarit Saliman/Dreamstime, Jeffrey Van Daele/Dreamstime

Printed in the United States of America

BE SAFE !

The experiments in this book are meant for kids to do themselves. Sometimes an adult's help is needed though. Look in the supply list for each experiment. It will list if an adult is needed. Also, some supplies will need to be bought by an adult.

TABLE OF CONTENTS

CHAPTER ONE
4 Study Simple Machines!

CHAPTER TWO
6 Seven Science Steps

CHAPTER THREE
8 Splitting Soap

CHAPTER FOUR
12 Up We Go!

CHAPTER FIVE
18 Easy Does It

CHAPTER SIX
24 Touch of a Finger

30 Glossary
32 Books and Web Sites
32 Index
32 About the Author

4

A crane uses different simple machines to lift heavy things.

Study Simple Machines!

Have you screwed in a light bulb? Have you seen a large crane at a construction site? It can lift very heavy things. Or have you pulled open window blinds with a cord? These seem like very different things. But they all use simple machines to make work easier.

What are simple machines? They are things that make lifting, pulling, and building things easier. Simple machines include **levers**, **pulleys**, **inclined planes**, **wedges**, **screws**, and the wheel and **axle**. How can you learn more about simple machines?

5

CHAPTER TWO

Seven Science Steps

Doing a science **experiment** is a fun way to discover new facts! An experiment follows steps to find answers to science questions. This book has experiments to help you learn about simple machines. You will follow the same seven steps in each experiment:

Seven Steps

1. Research: Figure out the facts before you get started.

2. Question: What do you want to learn?

3. Guess: Make a **prediction**. What do you think will happen in the experiment?

4. Gather: Find the supplies you need for your experiment.

5. Experiment: Follow the directions.

6. Review: Look at the results of the experiment.

7. Conclusion: The experiment is done. Now it is time to reach a **conclusion**. Was your prediction right?

Are you ready to become a scientist? Let's experiment to learn about simple machines!

CHAPTER THREE

Splitting Soap

A flat head screwdriver is a wedge.

A wedge is shaped like a V. The top of the wedge is wide. It comes down to a point. Learn what kinds of work a wedge can do.

Research the Facts

Here are a few. What other facts can you find?

- **Force** is put on the wide part of a wedge to make it work.
- Plows, flat head screwdrivers, and scissors are wedges.

Ask Questions

- How does a wedge make work easier?
- What does a wedge do?

8

Make a Prediction

Here are two examples:

- A wedge will split something into two pieces.
- A wedge will not split something. It will make a hole in something.

Gather Your Supplies!

- A flat head screwdriver
- A ruler
- 2 small bars of soap
- Newspaper
- Table
- Pencil or pen
- Paper

Time to Experiment!

1. Place the newspaper on a table. Place one small bar of soap on the newspaper.
2. Put the short end of the ruler on the middle of the soap. Push down on the ruler.
3. What happens? Did the soap split? Was it hard or easy to push down? Record in your notes what happens.
4. Put the tip of the screwdriver on the middle of the other soap. Push down on the screwdriver.
5. What happens? Was it hard or easy to push? Record what you see.

Review the Results

Read your notes. The soap did not split with the ruler. The soap split with the screwdriver.

What Is Your Conclusion?

The tip of the screwdriver is a wedge. You used force to push the screwdriver. A wedge is shaped to spread the force to the sides of an object. When you pushed on the screwdriver, it spread force on the sides of the soap. The soap split easily. The end of the ruler did not split the soap. The ruler is not a wedge. It took the force you used and just pushed straight down. The sides of the soap did not move.

An axe is a wedge. It splits wood into smaller pieces.

The cord on window blinds connects to a pulley.

CHAPTER FOUR

Up We Go!

Have you pulled down on a cord to lift up window blinds? There is a pulley in the blinds that helps you do this. A pulley is a wheel with a **groove** on its edges. Try this to see how a pulley works.

Research the Facts

Here are a few. What other facts do you know?

- A string or rope goes in a pulley's groove.
- Flag poles and cranes use pulleys.

Ask Questions

- What happens when you pull on a rope in a pulley?
- Do pulleys help us lift things?

Make a Prediction

Here are two examples:

- Pulling a rope on a pulley will make the other side go up.
- Pulling a rope on a pulley will make the other side go down.

13

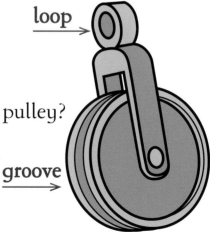

loop

groove

Gather Your Supplies!

- Adult help
- A 3-foot (1 m) length of clothesline
- A 6-foot (2 m) length of clothesline
- Clothesline pulley
- Tree with low limb
- Sandbox sand
- Small bucket with handle
- Pencil or pen
- Paper

Time to Experiment!

1. Put one 3-foot (1 m) length of clothesline through the loop at the top of the pulley.
2. Ask an adult to use that rope to tie the pulley to the tree limb.

3. Fill three-quarters of the small bucket with sand.

4. Tie an end of the other piece of clothesline to the handle of the small bucket. Put the bucket on the ground.

5. Ask an adult to pass the other end of the clothesline over the groove on the pulley.

6. Pull on the free end of the clothesline.

7. Record what happens.

Review the Results

What happened when you pulled on the clothesline? When you pulled down on the rope, the bucket lifted up into the air.

What Is Your Conclusion?

Using a pulley changes the direction of the force. This means that when you pull down on the rope, the bucket moves up, not down. A bucket with sand lifts up when using a pulley. The pulley reverses your force.

You can use pulleys to move objects up, down, or sideways.

Pulleys are used to raise the sails on sailboats.

Movers use ramps to move boxes into their trucks.

18

CHAPTER FIVE

Easy Does It!

Have you seen movers in action? They do not lift heavy boxes from the ground into their trucks. They use a ramp. A ramp is an inclined plane. Try this to see how an inclined plane works.

Research the Facts

Here are a few. What other facts can you find?

- An inclined plane is low at one end. It is higher on the other end.
- The top of an inclined plane is flat.

Ask Questions

- How do you use an inclined plane to do work?
- Does it matter if an inclined plane is short or long?

Make a Prediction

Here are two examples:

- An inclined plane needs to be long to work well.
- An inclined plane needs to be short to work well.

Gather Your Supplies!

- Large box with cover
- Yardstick
- 12-inch ruler
- Small box
- Rocks
- Tape
- Paper
- Pen or pencil

Time to Experiment!

1. Place the large box on the floor.
2. Place the small box beside the large box. Put the rocks in the small box. Tape it shut.

box and put it on the large box.

or hard it is to pick up the small box.

all box off of the large box.

12-inch ruler on the top edge of the large

end on the floor.

ox on the ruler. Push it up the ruler to the

ox.

or hard the box is to slide up.

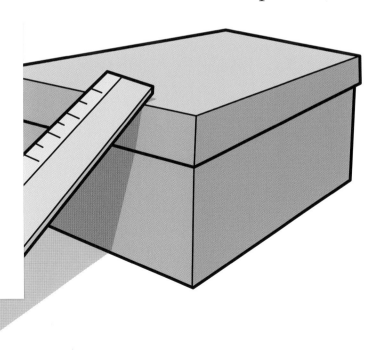

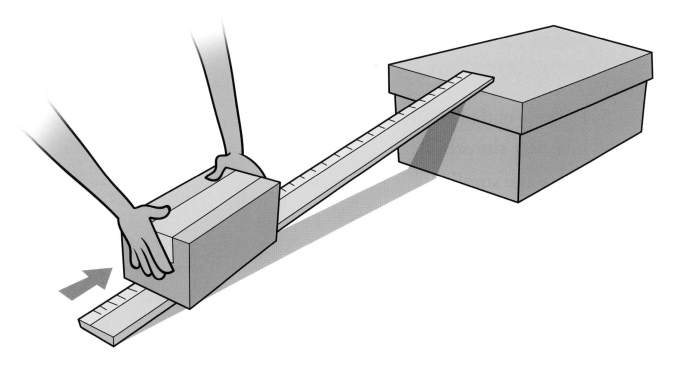

8. Remove the ruler. Now place the yardstick so one end is on the top edge of the large box. Put the other end on the floor.

9. Place the small box on the yardstick. Push it up the yardstick to the large box.

10. Record how easy or hard the small box is to slide up.

Review the Results

Read your notes. What did you notice? It was easier to lift the box using the ruler. It was even easier using the yardstick.

What Is Your Conclusion?

The ruler and yardstick were inclined planes. Using an inclined plane made it easier to move the small box. The yardstick was easiest to use. It took less force when the box went a longer distance. The ruler was a bit harder to use. It took more force to push up the shorter distance.

A screw is another simple machine. It is an inclined plane wrapped around a rod. Screws work well to hold things together. Look under the chair you are sitting on. It probably has a couple screws!

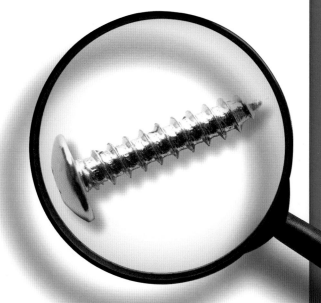

Seesaws go up and down.

24

CHAPTER SIX

Touch of a Finger

Have you ever played on a seesaw? When one end goes up, the other goes down. The seesaw is a lever. Learn how a lever works by doing this experiment.

Research the Facts

Here are a few. What other facts do you know?

- A lever moves up and down. It sits on a fixed point. This point is the **fulcrum**.
- A seesaw has the fulcrum in the middle of the lever. A fulcrum is not always at the middle of a lever, though.

Ask Questions

- Can a lever be used to move a heavy object?
- Does it matter where the fulcrum is placed on the lever?

Make a Prediction

Here are two examples:

- If the fulcrum is close to the object, it is hard to move the object.
- If the fulcrum is close to the object, it is easy to move the object.

Gather Your Supplies!

- Hardcover book
- Table
- 12-inch ruler
- Pink eraser (with straight, flat edges)
- Pencil or pen
- Paper

Time to Experiment!

1. Place the book on the table.
2. Put one finger under the edge of the book.
3. Lift the book with one finger.
4. Record if this is easy or hard to do.
5. Place the pink eraser on its long, flat edge.

6. Put the ruler on top of the eraser. Make sure the eraser is at the middle point of the ruler.

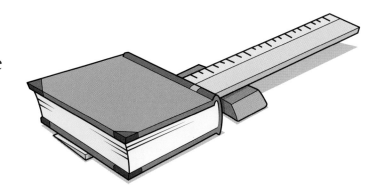

7. Put the book on one end of the ruler. The ruler's end will touch the table.

8. Use one finger to push on the other end of the ruler. Try to lift the book. Record if this is easy or hard to do.

9. Move the eraser closer to the book. Push on the ruler to try to lift the book. Record if this is easy or hard to do.

10. Move the eraser closer to your hand. Push on the ruler to try to lift the book. Record if this is easy or hard to do.

Review the Results

Read your notes. Was it easy or hard to use a lever? Did it matter where the fulcrum was? Did the lever help you move the book? It was easier to move the book when the eraser was closer to the book. It was harder to move the book when the eraser was closer to your hand.

What Is Your Conclusion?

The eraser was the fulcrum. The ruler was the lever. Using a lever made it easier to lift the book. Pushing down on one end of a lever makes the other end lift up. The closer the fulcrum was to the book, the easier it was to move the book.

A bottle opener and a hammer are also levers.

WAY TO GO!

You are a scientist now. What fun simple machine facts did you learn? You found out that simple machines make work easier. You saw that levers, pulleys, and inclined planes help you lift heavy things. You can learn even more about simple machines. Study them. Experiment with them. Then share what you learn about simple machines.

Glossary

axle (AK-suhl): An axle is the rod at the center of a wheel. An axle connects to two wheels.

conclusion (kuhn-KLOO-shuhn): A conclusion is what you learn from doing an experiment. Her conclusion is that a screw is a simple machine.

experiment (ek-SPER-uh-ment): An experiment is a test or way to study something to learn facts. This experiment showed the class that a pulley helps you lift things.

force (FORSS): A force is an action that changes an object's shape or how it moves. Simple machines help you use less force to do work.

fulcrum (FUL-kruhm): A fulcrum is the point on which a lever rests or turns. A seesaw sits on a fulcrum in the middle.

groove (GROOV): A groove is a long cut on the top of something. A pulley has a groove around its wheel.

inclined planes (in-KLINDE PLANEZ): Inclined planes are long, flat objects that lean on something so that one end is higher than the other end. Inclined planes are used to push things up.

levers (LEV-urz): Levers have a bar that sits on a fulcrum and can be used to lift heavy objects. Seesaws are levers.

prediction (pri-DIKT-shun): A prediction is what you think will happen in the future. His prediction is that a wedge splits things easily.

pulleys (PUL-eez): Pulleys have a wheel with a groove in which a rope or chain sits and that are used to lift loads. Window blinds use pulleys to lift up.

screws (SKROOZ): Screws have a lever wrapped around a rod and are used to hold two things together. Screws keep two wood pieces together.

wedges (WEJ-ez): Wedges are wide at one end and pointed at the other end and are used to split things apart. Axes are wedges.

Books

Deane-Pratt, Ade. *Simple Machines.* New York: PowerKids Press, 2012.

Gosman, Gillian. *Wedges in Action.* New York: PowerKids Press, 2011.

Monroe, Tilda. *What Do You Know About Simple Machines?* New York: Rosen, 2011.

Index

axe, 11
force, 8, 11, 16, 23
fulcrum, 25, 26, 28
hammer, 28
inclined plane, 5, 19, 23, 29
lever, 5, 25, 28, 29
pulley, 5, 13–16, 29

ramp, 19
screw, 5, 23
screwdriver, 8–11
seesaw, 25
wedge, 5, 8–9, 11
wheel and axle, 5

32

Web Sites

Visit our Web site for links about simple machine experiments:
childsworld.com/links

Note to Parents, Teachers, and Librarians: We routinely verify our Web links to make sure they are safe and active sites. So encourage your readers to check them out!

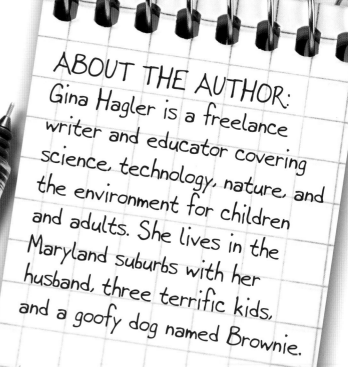

ABOUT THE AUTHOR:
Gina Hagler is a freelance writer and educator covering science, technology, nature, and the environment for children and adults. She lives in the Maryland suburbs with her husband, three terrific kids, and a goofy dog named Brownie.